Volume 2

FLUTE TRIOS

Editor: Trevor Wye

INDEX

			Page Score	Part
1.	Intrada	Franck	2	1
2.	Courante	Praetorius	3	1
3.	A Prelude	Mattheson	4	2
4.	Introduction and Air	Finger	6	2
5.	Allemande	Boismortier	8	3
6.	Courante	Boismortier	10	4
7	Minuet	Finger	12	4
8.	Trio in A Minor	Kummer	13	5
9.	Romance	Krommer	17	6
10.	Rondeau	Boismortier	20	7
11.	Gigue	Boismortier	22	8
12.	Minuet and Trio in F	Kuhlau	24	9
	Notes on the composers		28	

This is a performing score which should be used by Flute 1.
Separate parts are provided for Flute 2 and Flute 3.

CHESTER MUSIC

FLUTE TRIOS
Volume II
Selected and edited by TREVOR WYE

I. Intrada

FRANCK

* N.B. as in the previous volume, a drum or tambourine part can be added if desired.

CH55189

2. Courante

PRAETORIUS
Allegro (♩ = 132)
I
II
III
f-p
*Drum or Tambourine:

*Drum or
Tambourine:

3. A Prelude

MATTHESON

* *Trills*: Play the upper note only as long as indicated and *always on* the beat.

The last bar should be played as follows:—   This formula can be applied to most 18th century trills.

4. Introduction and Air

Introduction

FINGER

*~ *is a mordent*. It is like the first 3 notes of a trill. Just let your finger bounce *once* on the key. Do play a *double mordent*, if you prefer it. i.e. the first 5 notes of a trill. Throughout the rest of this book, play a mordent, a double mordent, or even a short trill whenever you see a cross over a note. i.e. +. Play whichever sounds best; this is what flute players did in the 18th century.

5. Allemande

BOISMORTIER

13
f
p
f
p
f
p
17
mf
mf
mf
21
p
p
p
25
cresc.
f
cresc.
f
cresc.
f
rit. 2nd. time
28
p
p
p

6. Courante

BOISMORTIER

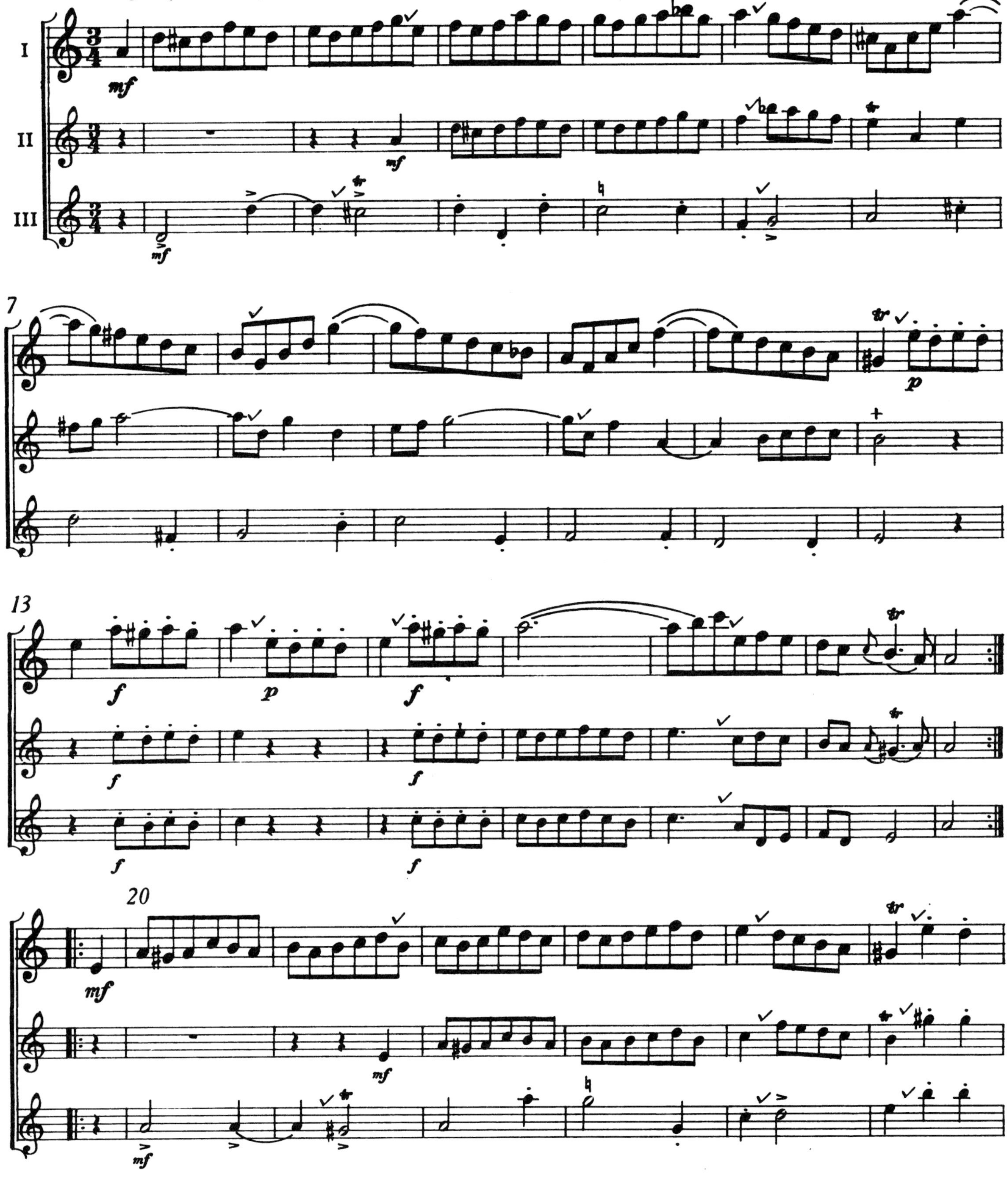

7. Minuet

FINGER

8. Trio in A minor

KUMMER

28
31
34
36
poco rit.
f
p
f
p
p
p
p

39 a tempo
Solo
43
47
50 dim. e rit.

9. Romance

Andante ♩ = 100
KROMMER
I
II
III
p
delicato
fz
cantabile
sim.
8va
mf
pp

25
30
cresc.
cresc.
cresc.
f
p
f
3
35
rit.
a tempo
p
f
p
40
p
fz
p
fz
p
fz
45
f
sim.
fz
sim.
fz
sim.
tr

10. Rondeau

BOISMORTIER

II. Gigue

BOISMORTIER

* ♦ This is an *inverted* (or upside down) *mordent*. It has 3 notes (like an ordinary mordent) but the second note goes *down* instead of up. Where inverted mordents are marked, try a *double* inverted mordent (5 notes) and play whichever sounds the best. All mordents are, of course, played *on* the beat.

12. Minuet and Trio in F

from Op. 13, No. 3

N.B. Fl. II turns back from Trio and over for Coda.

MINUET Allegro assai ($\quad$ = 152)

KUHLAU

This is the classic form of the symphonic minuet: make both repeats in the minuet, both repeats in the trio (a little slower), then play the minuet without repeats, at the end of which play the coda to finish.

24
p
p
(7)
p
30
f
f
f
36
p
cresc.
p
cresc.
p
cresc.
42
dim.
f
Last time to Coda
Turn over to Coda for Fl. I
p
f
p
f

TRIO

TRIO
(♩ = 138)
I
II
III
pp
pp
pp
7
14
21
Da Capo al Minuet
Turn back for Fl. I on D.C. Minuet.

CODA

NOTES ON THE COMPOSERS

Joseph Bodin de Boismortier (1691 -1755)
A French composer who wrote much chamber music for the flute.

Godfrey Finger (c.1660-c.1732)
A Moravian composer. He lived in England for 15 years during which he wrote music for the London stage and many chamber works.

Melchior Franck (1573-1639)
A German composer, he held the post of Kapellmeister to the Duke of Coburg from 1603 until his death.

Franz Krommer (1759-1831)
An Austrian composer, Krommer was strongly influenced by Mozart and Haydn. Towards the end of his life he enjoyed many honours and successes.

Frederich Kuhlau (1787-1832)
Born in Hanover, he had the misfortune to lose an eye whilst a child, but this did not prevent him from becoming a brilliant pianist and flute player. He was a close friend of Beethoven.

Gaspard Kummer (1795-1870)
A flautist and composer of numerous works for the flute.

Johann Mattheson (1681-1764)
Mattheson showed unusual talent at an early age. At the end of his schooling he was said to be good at classics, proficient in modern languages, a student of both law and political science, a fine player on harpsichord and organ, thoroughly skilled in musical theory, an elegant dancer and a master at fencing!

Michael Praetorius (1571-1621)
A composer and organist to the Duke of Brunswick.

FLUTE TRIOS

Editor: Trevor Wye

INDEX

			Page	
			Score	Part
1.	Intrada	Franck	2	1
2.	Courante	Praetorius	3	1
3.	A Prelude	Mattheson	4	2
4.	Introduction and Air	Finger	6	2
5.	Allemande	Boismortier	8	3
6.	Courante	Boismortier	10	4
7	Minuet	Finger	12	4
8.	Trio in A Minor	Kummer	13	5
9.	Romance	Krommer	17	6
10.	Rondeau	Boismortier	20	7
11.	Gigue	Boismortier	22	8
12.	Minuet and Trio in F	Kuhlau	24	9
	Notes on the composers		28	

CHESTER MUSIC

FLUTE TRIOS
Volume II
Selected and edited by TREVOR WYE

1. Intrada

FRANCK

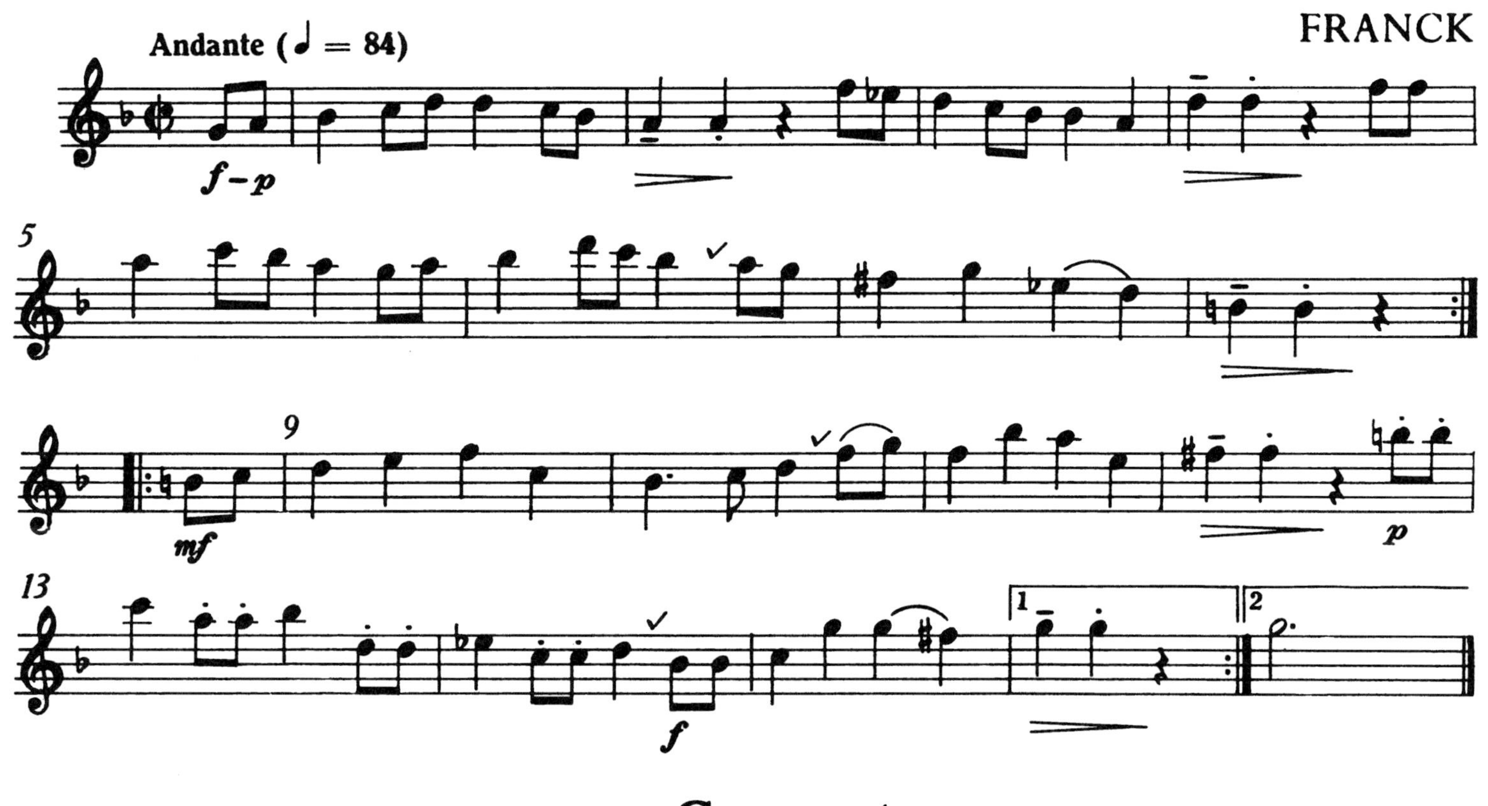

2. Courante

PRAETORIUS

3. A Prelude

MATTHESON

***** *Trills* : Play the upper note only as long as indicated and *always on* the beat. The last bar should be played as follows : -
This formula can be applied to most 18th century trills.

4. Introduction and Air
Introduction

FINGER

***~** *is a mordent.* It is like the first 3 notes of a trill. Just let your finger bounce *once* on the key. Do play a *double mordent,* if you prefer it. i.e. the first 5 notes of a trill. Throughout the rest of this book, play a mordent, a double mordent, or even a short trill whenever you see a cross over a note. i.e. **+**. Play whichever sounds best ; this is what flute players did in the 18th century.

17
25
p
33
mf
f
p
f

5. Allemande
BOISMORTIER
Moderato (♩ = 76)
f
4
p
7
cresc.
f
10
p [echo]
13
f
p
18
mf
23
p
cresc.
f
27
rit. 2nd. time
p

6. Courante

BOISMORTIER

7. Minuet

FINGER

8. Trio in A minor

KUMMER

Andante (♪ = 120)

9. Romance

KROMMER

10. Rondeau

BOISMORTIER

II. Gigue

* This is an *inverted* (or upside down) *mordent*, It has 3 notes (like an ordinary mordent) but the second note goes *down* instead of up. Where inverted mordents are marked, try a *double* inverted mordent (5 notes) and play whichever sounds the best. All mordents are, of course, played *on* the beat.

12. Minuet and Trio in F
from Op. 13, No. 3

KUHLAU

Flute Editor: Trevor Wye   Clarinet Editor: Thea King

Oboe Editor: James Brown   Bassoon Editor: William Waterhouse

A growing collection of volumes from Chester Music, containing a wide range of pieces from different periods.

FLUTE SOLOS VOLUME I

Baston	Siciliana from Concertino in D
Blavet	Gavotte—La Dédale
Bochsa	Nocturne
Buchner	Russian Melody from Fantasy op. 22
Eichner	Minuet from Sonata No. 6
Franck	Intrada
Franck	Galliard
Lichtenthal	Theme
Mozart	Minuets I & II from Sonata No. 1
Paisiello	Nel Cor Più
Vivaldi	Andante from Sonata No. 3 of The Faithful Shepherd
Vivaldi	Pastorale from Sonata No. 4 of The Faithful Shepherd

FLUTE SOLOS VOLUME II

Blavet	Les Tendres Badinages from Sonata No. 6
Chopin	A Rossini Theme
Donjon	Adagio Nobile
Eichner	Scherzando from Sonata No. 6
Harmston	Andante
Jacob	Cradle Song from Five Pieces for Harmonica and Piano
Mozart	Minuets I & II from Sonata No. 5
Mozart	Allegro from Sonata in G
Pauli	Capriccio
Telemann	Tempo Giusto from Sonata in D minor
Vivaldi	Allegro from Sonata No. 6 of The Faithful Shepherd

FLUTE SOLOS VOLUME III

Blavet	Sicilienne from Sonata No. 4
Blavet	Les Regrets from Sonata No. 5
Donjon	Offertoire op. 12
Eichner	Allegro from Sonata No. 6
Kelly	Jig from Serenade
Loeillet	Gavotte and Aria from Sonata No. 7
Nørgard	Andantino—Pastorale
Sibelius	Solo from Scaramouche op. 71
Telemann	Grave from Sonata in G minor
Vivaldi	Largo from Sonata No. 6 of The Faithful Shepherd

CHESTER MUSIC

FLUTE TRIOS

Editor: Trevor Wye

INDEX

			Page Score	Part
1.	Intrada	Franck	2	1
2.	Courante	Praetorius	3	1
3.	A Prelude	Mattheson	4	2
4.	Introduction and Air	Finger	6	2
5.	Allemande	Boismortier	8	3
6.	Courante	Boismortier	10	4
7	Minuet	Finger	12	4
8.	Trio in A Minor	Kummer	13	5
9.	Romance	Krommer	17	6
10.	Rondeau	Boismortier	20	7
11.	Gigue	Boismortier	22	8
12.	Minuet and Trio in F	Kuhlau	24	9
	Notes on the composers		28	

CHESTER MUSIC

FLUTE TRIOS
Volume II
Selected and edited by TREVOR WYE

1. Intrada

FRANCK

2. Courante

PRAETORIUS

3. A Prelude

MATTHESON

4. Introduction and Air

Introduction

FINGER

Air

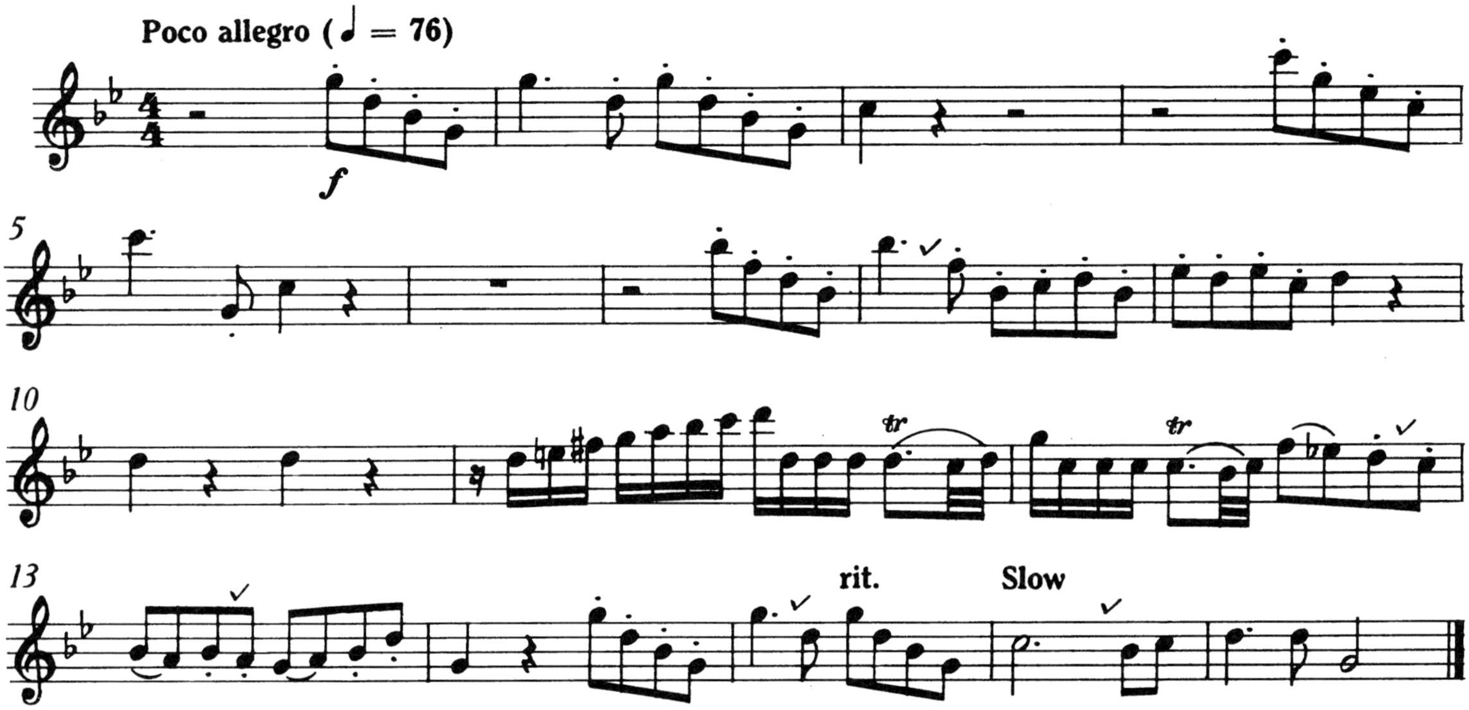

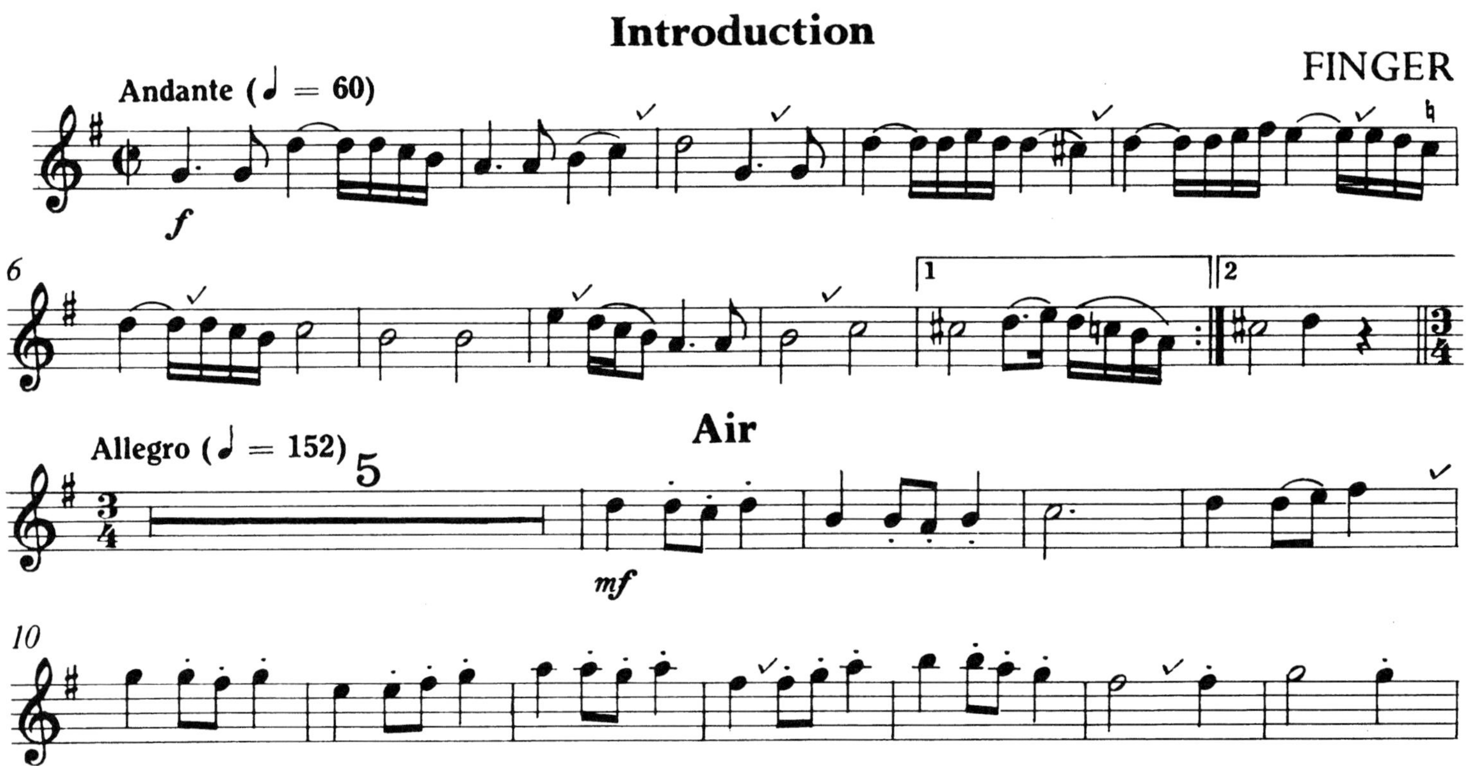

*～ _is a mordent_. It is like the first 3 notes of a trill. Just let your finger bounce _once_ on the key. Do play a _double mordent_, if you prefer it. i.e. the first 5 notes of a trill. Throughout the rest of this book, play a mordent, a double mordent, or even a short trill whenever you see a cross over a note. i.e. +. Play whichever sounds best; this is what flute players did in the 18th century.

5. Allemande

BOISMORTIER

Moderato (♩ = 76)

6. Courante

BOISMORTIER

7. Minuet

FINGER

8. Trio in A minor

KUMMER

9. Romance

KROMMER

10. Rondeau

BOISMORTIER

11. Gigue

BOISMORTIER

* This is an *inverted* (or upside down) *mordent*. It has 3 notes (like an ordinary mordent) but the second note goes *down* instead of up. Where inverted mordents are marked, try a *double* inverted mordent (5 notes) and play whichever sounds the best. All mordents are, of course, played *on* the beat.

12. Minuet and Trio in F

from Op. 13, No. 3

KUHLAU

Flute   Editor: Trevor Wye   Clarinet   Editor: Thea King
Oboe   Editor: James Brown   Bassoon   Editor: William Waterhouse

A growing collection of volumes from Chester Music, containing a
wide range of pieces from different periods.

FLUTE SOLOS VOLUME I

Baston	Siciliana from Concertino in D
Blavet	Gavotte—La Dédale
Bochsa	Nocturne
Buchner	Russian Melody from Fantasy op. 22
Eichner	Minuet from Sonata No. 6
Franck	Intrada
Franck	Galliard
Lichtenthal	Theme
Mozart	Minuets I & II from Sonata No. 1
Paisiello	Nel Cor Più
Vivaldi	Andante from Sonata No. 3 of The Faithful Shepherd
Vivaldi	Pastorale from Sonata No. 4 of The Faithful Shepherd

FLUTE SOLOS VOLUME II

Blavet	Les Tendres Badinages from Sonata No. 6
Chopin	A Rossini Theme
Donjon	Adagio Nobile
Eichner	Scherzando from Sonata No. 6
Harmston	Andante
Jacob	Cradle Song from Five Pieces for Harmonica and Piano
Mozart	Minuets I & II from Sonata No. 5
Mozart	Allegro from Sonata in G
Pauli	Capriccio
Telemann	Tempo Giusto from Sonata in D minor
Vivaldi	Allegro from Sonata No. 6 of The Faithful Shepherd

FLUTE SOLOS VOLUME III

Blavet	Sicilienne from Sonata No. 4
Blavet	Les Regrets from Sonata No. 5
Donjon	Offertoire op. 12
Eichner	Allegro from Sonata No. 6
Kelly	Jig from Serenade
Loeillet	Gavotte and Aria from Sonata No. 7
Nørgard	Andantino—Pastorale
Sibelius	Solo from Scaramouche op. 71
Telemann	Grave from Sonata in G minor
Vivaldi	Largo from Sonata No. 6 of The Faithful Shepherd

CHESTER MUSIC